W9-CMI-804

NIAGARA FALLS PUBLIC LIBRARY

COMMUNITY CENTRE BRANCH LIBRARY

A Note to Parents and Teachers

Kids can imagine, kids can laugh and kids can learn to read with this exciting new series of first readers. Each book in the Kids Can Read series has been especially written, illustrated and designed for beginning readers. Humorous, easy-to-read stories, appealing characters, and engaging illustrations make for books that kids will want to read over and over again.

To make selecting a book easy for kids, parents and teachers, the Kids Can Read series offers three levels based on different reading abilities:

Level 1: Kids Can Start to Read

Short stories, simple sentences, easy vocabulary, lots of repetition and visual clues for kids just beginning to read.

Level 2: Kids Can Read with Help

Longer stories, varied sentences, increased vocabulary, some repetition and visual clues for kids who have some reading skills, but may need a little help.

Level 3: Kids Can Read Alone

Longer, more complex stories and sentences, more challenging vocabulary, language play, minimal repetition and visual clues for kids who are reading by themselves.

With the Kids Can Read series, kids can enter a new and exciting world of reading!

Sam Goes to School

Written by **Mary Labatt**

Illustrated by **Marisol Sarrazin**

Kids Can Press

Sam was bored.

She looked out the window.

Kids were coming

down the street.

A big yellow bus came.

"Kids are going

on that bus!" thought Sam.

"I want to go, too!"

Sam ran to the door

and pushed.

It was open!

"Here I go!" she thought.

Sam ran to the bus.

Kids got on the bus.

Sam got on, too.

Sam hid under a seat.

A girl looked down.

"A puppy!" she said.

"Don't tell!" said a boy.

"We can take this puppy to school!"

The girl put Sam in her backpack.

"Hide in here, puppy," she said.

"This is good," thought Sam.

"I am going to school."

The girl closed the backpack.

"Shhh," she said.

The bus stopped

and the kids got out.

The kids went into the school.

Bump, bump, bump went Sam

inside the backpack.

The girl opened the backpack.

"Stay here, puppy," she said.

"Here is a cookie."

"Yum," thought Sam.

"School is fun!"

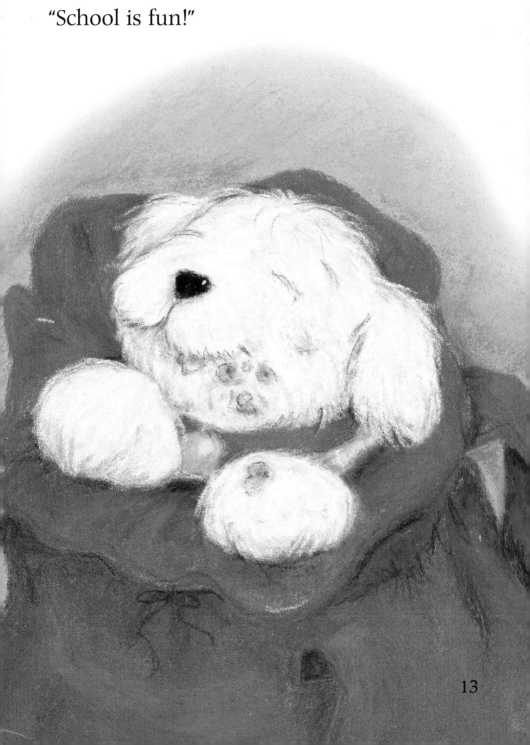

All morning the girl and boy

came to see Sam.

They gave Sam a sandwich,

some chips and a little cake.

But Sam got tired of the backpack.

"It is too dark in here," she thought.

"I am getting out."

Sam climbed out of the backpack

and peeked around the corner.

Sam saw lots of kids.

Kids were painting.

Kids were writing.

Kids were reading books.

The girl saw Sam.

"Oh, no!" she said.

"Oh, no!" said the boy.

But it was too late.

"I can paint with the kids," thought Sam.

She stepped in the paint

and walked all over the paintings.

"Oh, no!" said the kids.

"I can write with the kids," thought Sam.

She grabbed a paper.

Then she ripped it up.

"Oh, no!" said the kids.

"I can read with the kids," thought Sam.

She pulled a book off the shelf.

Then she chewed on it.

"Oh, no!" said the kids.

Miss Min came running.

"No, no, no!" she cried.

Miss Min picked Sam up

and looked at her tag.

"This is Sam," she said.

"Here is her phone number."

"I have to call Sam's family," said Miss Min.

"And we have to clean up Sam's mess."

Miss Min put Sam in a box.

"Sam can watch us

until her family comes," she said.

"No more painting for Sam."

Sam watched the kids.

Kids were writing.

Kids were painting.

Kids were reading books.

And kids were petting her!

Then Joan and Bob ran in.

"Sam!" cried Joan.

"How did you get here?"

"She came on the bus," said the girl.

"Woof!" said Sam.

"On the bus!" said Bob.

"The bus is not for puppies!"

"No," said Miss Min.

"Dogs cannot come to school."

29

"No dogs in school!" thought Sam.

"That is not fair!

School has kids.

School has painting.

School has cookies.

School has chips and cake!"

"Puppies need school, too!"

Text © 2004 Mary Labatt
Illustrations © 2004 Marisol Sarrazin

All rights reserved. No part of this publication may be reproduced,
stored in a retrieval system or transmitted, in any form or by any
means, without the prior written permission of Kids Can Press Ltd. or,
in case of photocopying or other reprographic copying, a license from
The Canadian Copyright Licensing Agency (Access Copyright). For an
Access Copyright license, visit www.accesscopyright.ca or call toll free
to 1-800-893-5777.

Kids Can Press acknowledges the financial support of the Government
of Ontario, through the Media Development Corporation's Ontario
Book Initiative; the Ontario Arts Council; the Canada Council for the
Arts; and the Government of Canada, through the BPIDP, for our
publishing activity.

Published in Canada by
Kids Can Press Ltd.
29 Birch Avenue
Toronto, ON M4V 1E2

Published in the U.S. by
Kids Can Press Ltd.
2250 Military Road
Tonawanda, NY 14150

www.kidscanpress.com

Edited by David MacDonald
Designed by Marie Bartholomew
Printed in Hong Kong, China, by Book Art Inc., Toronto

The hardcover edition of this book is smyth sewn casebound.
The paperback edition of this book is limp sewn with a drawn-on cover.

CM 04 0 9 8 7 6 5 4 3 2 1
CM PA 04 0 9 8 7 6 5 4 3 2 1

National Library of Canada Cataloguing in Publication Data

Labatt, Mary, [date]

  Sam goes to school / written by Mary Labatt ; illustrated by
Marisol Sarrazin.

(Kids Can read)
ISBN 1-55337-564-5 (bound).   ISBN 1-55337-565-3 (pbk.)

I. Sarrazin, Marisol, 1965– II. Title. III. Series: Kids Can read
(Toronto, Ont.)

PS8573.A135S244 2004   jC813'.54   C2003-902331-1
PZ7

Kids Can Press is a *l'ОГ'US*™ Entertainment company

NIAGARA FALLS PUBLIC LIBRARY

COMMUNITY CENTRE BRANCH LIBRARY

MAY - - 2005